For Marcelo
G.K.

For my parents
N.V.

MARC

First American edition 2004
by Kane/Miller Book Publishers, Inc.
La Jolla, California

First published in 2001 by Editorial Kókinos, Spain
Text copyright © Gabriela Keselman, 2001
Illustrations copyright © Noemí Villamuza, 2001

Library of Congress Control Number: 2004100984

Printed and bound in China by Regent Publishing Services Ltd.

1 2 3 4 5 6 7 8 9 10

ISBN 1-929132-68-9

Gabriela Keselman ∾ Noemí Villamuza

JUST COULDN'T SLEEP

Kane/Miller
BOOK PUBLISHERS

Marc wanted to go to sleep.
Really, he did.
But he couldn't.
He just couldn't sleep.

He called out for his mom.

"I'm afraid a giant mosquito will fly in and bite me," he said.

"Don't worry little one," his mom answered. "I'll fix that, and soon you'll be sound asleep."

She made him a special pair of mosquito-proof pajamas complete with a helmet, a sword for protecting himself, and a buzz-repellent teddy bear.

And then she left.

Soon Marc called out for his mom again. "I'm afraid I'll fall out of bed," he told her.

"Don't worry my love," his mom answered. "I'll fix that, and you'll soon drift off to sleep."

She gave him a mountain climbing rope, secured it to his pillow with an anchor, and slipped a parachute over his back.

And then she left.

Shortly afterwards Marc called out once more. "What if the moon melts, and the world goes dark?" he asked.

"Don't worry honey," his mom answered, "I'll fix that, and soon you'll fall fast asleep." She gave him a pair of glasses with glow in the dark lenses and sent a letter to the moon. The letter said, "Moon, don't even think about doing anything silly like melting or something."

And then she left.

A few minutes later Marc called out yet again.

"I'm afraid a mean wind will blow in my face, and I'll catch cold," he told his mom.

"Don't worry darling," his mom answered. "I'll fix that, and you'll fall asleep so easily."

She hung a sign on the front door of the house that said, "Mean wind, you took the wrong road. Buy yourself a map!" She covered Marc with ten goose feathers and a real live duck.

And then she left.

Finally, Marc called to his mom one last time.

"I think I'm afraid of everything," he said.

"Don't worry sweetheart," answered his mom. "I'll fix all of that, and you'll sleep soundly through the night."
She began running around the house. She closed doors, windows, suitcases, and notebooks. She scared away all the monsters and witches; she even scared away the dentist and all the relatives. She invented a special stick for fighting off nightmares and an invisible trap for catching ghosts.

And even though it wasn't really necessary, she went up to the roof to keep watch, just in case.

But suddenly she heard Marc's voice.

Marc's mom, exhausted from trying to find the right solution, came down from the roof.

She took off Marc's mosquito-proof armor.

She unfastened his mountain climbing equipment.

She ripped up the letters to the moon and the mean wind.

She sent the duck off to have a bath.

She took away the traps and the sticks.

And then finally, she sat down on her son's bed. She ruffled his hair and said, "My dear, I really don't know what else I can do to help you stop feeling so afraid. I think I'll just have to sit here next to you and you can tell me everything."

Smiling and yawning at the same time, Marc took his mom's hands and whispered, "I'll tell you later, I'm much too tired now..."

Marc wanted to stay awake.
Really, he did.
But he couldn't.
He just couldn't stay awake.

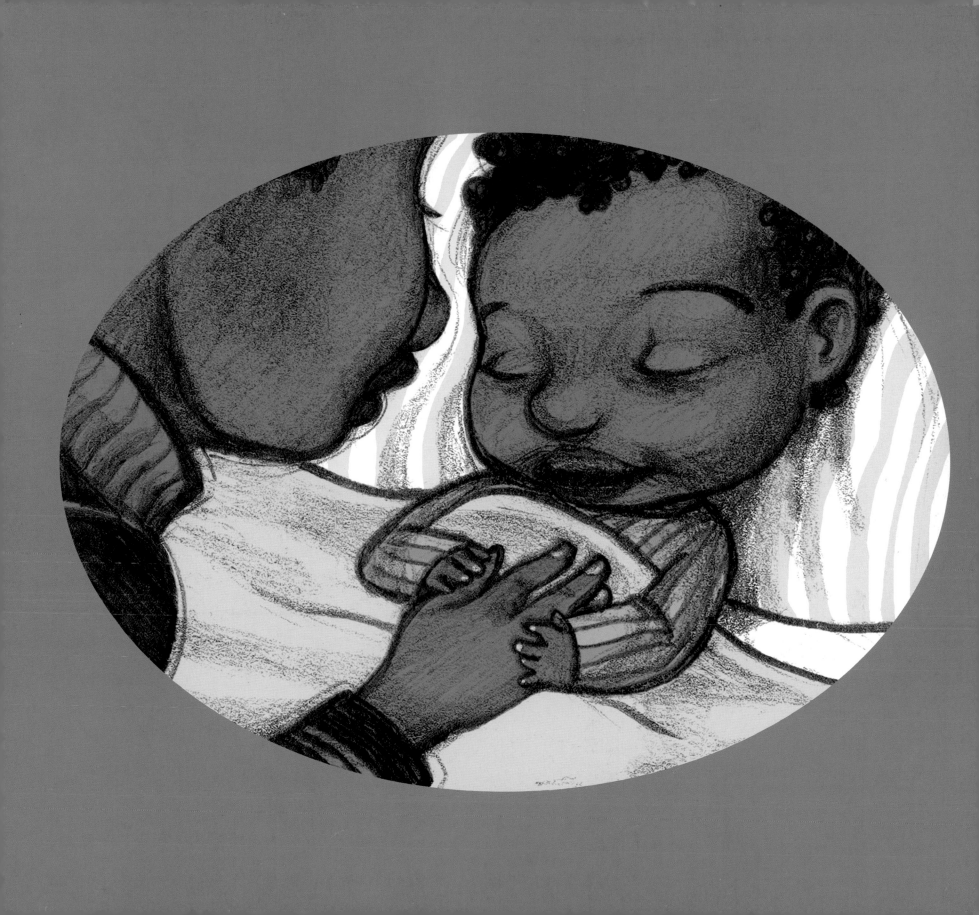

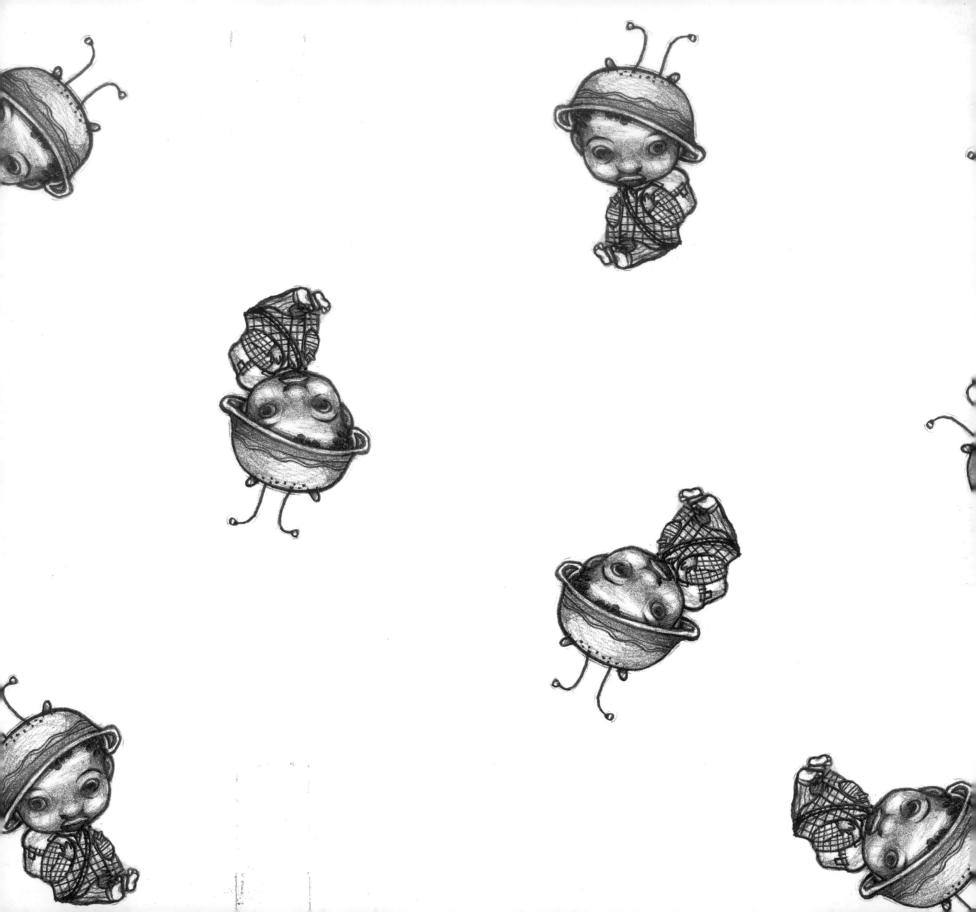